Noisy Nora

WITH ALL NEW ILLUSTRATIONS
ROSEMARY WELLS

DOUBLEDAY
London New York Toronto Sydney Auckland

TRANSWORLD PUBLISHERS LTD
61-63 Uxbridge Road, London W5 5SA

TRANSWORLD PUBLISHERS (AUSTRALIA) PTY LTD
15-25 Helles Avenue, Moorebank, NSW 2170

TRANSWORLD PUBLISHERS (NZ) LTD
3 William Pickering Drive, Albany, Auckland

DOUBLEDAY CANADA LTD
105 Bond Street, Toronto, Ontario M5B lY3

First published in the United States in 1997 by Dial Books for Young Readers
Published in Great Britain in 1998 by Doubleday
a division of Transworld Publishers Ltd

Copyright © Rosemary Wells 1998

The right of Rosemary Wells to be identified as the Author
of this work has been asserted in accordance with
the Copyright, Designs and Patents Act l988

A catalogue record for this book is available
from the British Library

ISBN 0 385 40948 6

Printed in Belgium by Proost Book Productions

For Joan Read

Jack had dinner early,

Father played with Kate,

Jack needed burping,
So Nora had to wait.

First she banged the window,

Then she slammed the door,

Then she dropped her sister's marbles
on the kitchen floor.

"Quiet!" said her father.
"Hush!" said her mum.

"Nora!" said her sister,
"Why are you so dumb?"

Jack had gotten filthy,

Mother cooked with Kate,

Jack needed drying off,
So Nora had to wait.

First she knocked the lamp down,
Then she felled some chairs,

Then she took her brother's kite

And flew it down the stairs.

"Quiet!" said her father.
"Hush!" said her mum.

"Nora!" said her sister.
"Why are you so dumb?"

Jack was getting sleepy,

Father read with Kate,

Jack needed singing to,
So Nora had to wait.

"I'm leaving!" shouted Nora,
"And I'm never coming back!"

And they didn't hear a sound
But a tralala from Jack.

Father stopped his reading.
Mother stopped her song.

"Mercy!" said her sister,
"Something's very wrong."

No Nora in the cellar.
No Nora in the tub.

No Nora in the mail box
Or hiding in a shrub.

"She's left us!" moaned her mother
As they sifted through the trash.

"But I'm back again!" said Nora

With a monumental crash.